Romeo & Juliet

Artists: Penko Gelev
Sotir Gelev

First edition for North America (including Canada and Mexico),
Philippine Islands, and Puerto Rico published in 2009
by Barron's Educational Series, Inc.

All inquiries should be addressed to:
Barron's Educational Series, Inc.
250 Wireless Boulevard
Hauppauge, NY 11788
www.barronseduc.com

ISBN-13 (Hardcover): 978-0-7641-6244-2
ISBN-10 (Hardcover): 0-7641-6244-6
ISBN-13 (Paperback): 978-0-7641-4277-2
ISBN-10 (Paperback): 0-7641-4277-1

Library of Congress Control No.: 2009925458

Printed on paper from sustainable sources.

Picture credits:
p 40: TopFoto.co.uk
p 41: John James
Every effort has been made to trace copyright holders. The Salariya Book Company apologizes for
any omissions and would be pleased, in such cases, to add an acknowledgement in future editions.

Printed and bound in China
9 8 7 6 5 4 3 2 1

Romeo & Juliet

William Shakespeare

Illustrated by

Penko Gelev

Retold by

Jim Pipe

Series created and designed by

David Salariya

O Romeo, Romeo, wherefore art thou Romeo? Deny thy father and refuse thy name, or if thou wilt not, be but sworn my love, and I'll no longer be a Capulet. (*see page 19*).

CHARACTERS

Romeo

Juliet

Mercutio,
Romeo's friend

Tybalt, Juliet's cousin

Friar Laurence

Nurse

Lord Capulet, Juliet's father

Lady Capulet, Juliet's
mother

Lord Montague,
Romeo's father

Lady Montague,
Romeo's mother

Paris

Benvolio,
Romeo's cousin

Escalus, Prince of
Verona

TWO FAMILIES AT WAR

In Verona, a town in northern Italy, two noble families, the Montagues and the Capulets, are at war because of an ancient grudge.[1]

From these houses, two star-crossed[2] young lovers will mend the quarrel between their families by falling in love – and dying. Read on to find out how their tragic story unfolds...

All seems quiet in Verona's busy public square.

> Draw thy tool! Here come members of the house of Montague.[3]

> My naked weapon is out: quarrel,[4] I will back thee.

However, two Capulets, Sampson and Gregory, are hungry for a fight.

> Do you bite your thumb[5] at us, sir?

> No, sir, I do not bite my thumb at you, sir, but I bite my thumb, sir.

They run into Abraham and Balthasar, two Montagues. Sampson tries to provoke Abraham by making a rude gesture.

> Do you quarrel, sir?

> Quarrel, sir? No, sir.

The men know they should not argue in a public place, but Abraham quickly rises to the bait.

> I serve as good a man as you.

> No better.

Sampson claims the Capulets are better than the Montagues.

> Yes, better, sir.

> You lie.

> Draw,[6] if you be men.

> A fight breaks out...

1. grudge: feeling of resentment.
2. star-crossed: ill-fated.
3. "Draw thy tool . . . Montagues." Unsheathe your sword. Here come members of the Montague household.
4. quarrel: start an argument.
5. bite your thumb: a rude gesture, done by flicking your thumb out from behind your front teeth.
6. draw: pull out your sword.

THE PRINCE'S WARNING

Benvolio,[1] a Montague, arrives and tries to separate the angry men.

Just then, Tybalt, Lord Capulet's hot-headed nephew, joins the men. Spoiling for a fight, he draws his sword on Benvolio.

Benvolio tries to calm things down. But Tybalt causes trouble.

Tybalt attacks Benvolio.

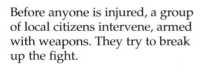

Before anyone is injured, a group of local citizens intervene, armed with weapons. They try to break up the fight.

Hearing the noise, Lord Capulet rushes to join in. Lady Capulet mocks her aged husband.

On the opposite side of the piazza, Lady Montague also tries to restrain her husband.

---

8   1. Benvolio's name means "well-wisher."   2. drawn: with your sword in your hand.   3. have at thee: on guard!
4. bills and partisans: two types of pike – hooked spears at the end of a long pole.   5. crutch: walking aid.

Rebellious subjects, enemies to peace!

Throw your mistempered[1] weapons to the ground.

Three civil brawls,[2] bred of an airy[3] word...

... have thrice[4] disturbed the quiet of our streets.

Suddenly, Prince Escalus, the ruler of Verona, steps in to halt the violence. He is tired of the disruptions caused by the two feuding families.

Seeing the Prince and his soldiers, the Montagues and Capulets stop fighting. The Prince is furious: it's the third time they've fought on the streets of Verona.

If ever you disturb our streets again, your lives shall pay the forfeit[5] of the peace.

Later...

O, where is Romeo? Saw you him today?

Underneath the grove of sycamore... So early walking did I see your son.

The Prince issues a stern warning: any Capulets and Montagues caught fighting will be executed.

Reluctantly, the Capulets and Montagues leave the piazza, but the tension between the two families remains.

Lord and Lady Montague ask Benvolio if he has seen their son Romeo. Romeo has been acting strangely recently.

Many a morning he has been there seen...

My noble uncle, do you know the cause?

Could we but learn from whence[7] his sorrows grow, we would as willingly give cure as know.

...with tears augmenting[6] the fresh morning's dew.

I neither know it nor can learn of him.

Lord Montague has tried to find out why Romeo is so depressed, but his son keeps his feelings to himself.

1. mistempered: wrongly made or "tempered," because they are being used by people in a bad temper.   2. brawls: fights.
3. airy: vague – no one knows exactly why the Montagues and Capulets are fighting.   4. thrice: three times.
5. forfeit: penalty for breaking the peace.   6. augmenting: adding to.   7. whence: from what cause.

LOVESTRUCK ROMEO

Good morrow,[1] cousin.

Is the day so young?

Benvolio runs into Romeo in a sidestreet. Benvolio asks why his friend is looking so upset.

What sadness lengthens Romeo's hours?

Not having that which, having, makes them short.[2]

In love?

Out…

Of love?

Out of her favor where I am in love.

Tell me in sadness,[3] who is it that you love?

In sadness, cousin, I do love a woman.

Romeo confides that he is in love with a girl, Rosaline, who does not return his affections.

Be ruled by me;[4] forget to think of her.

Oh, teach me how I should forget to think!

By giving liberty unto thine eyes.[5] Examine other beauties.

Benvolio advises Romeo to forget Rosaline and find another woman.

Farewell. Thou canst not[6] teach me to forget.

Romeo isn't convinced – he believes he will never forget Rosaline's beauty.

10   1. morrow: morning.   2. Not having… short: Not having the thing that makes time pass quickly.
3. in sadness: seriously.   4. Be ruled by me: Take my advice.   5. By giving liberty unto thine eyes:
Allow your eyes to wander.   6. Thou canst not: You can't.

'Tis not hard, I think, for men so old as we to keep the peace.

Meanwhile...

Paris, a relative of the Prince of Verona, is talking to Lord Capulet. Paris hopes to marry Lord Capulet's daughter, Juliet.

Lord Capulet knows both he and Lord Montague are troubled by the latest fight between their young relatives.

But now, my lord, what say you to my suit?[1]

My child is yet a stranger in the world. She hath not seen the change of fourteen years.[2]

Younger than she are happy mothers made.

Paris nods in agreement, but he's keen to talk about his marriage to Juliet.

Lord Capulet is annoyed by Paris' impatience. He feels Juliet is too young to marry.

Capulet wants Paris to wait two more years, but Paris protests – girls younger than Juliet are mothers.[3]

But woo her, gentle Paris, get her heart.

This night I hold an old accustomed feast.

Come, go with me.

Lord Capulet reminds Paris he has to win Juliet over before he will agree to their marriage.

Capulet invites Paris to a masquerade[4] he is holding that night, in the hope that Paris will capture Juliet's heart.

1. suit: marriage proposal.   2. She hath… fourteen years: she isn't even 14 yet.
3. mothers: in those times, 13-year-old girls were often married with children.
4. masquerade: a ball where the guests wear masks.

AN INVITATION TO THE FEAST

Find those persons out whose names are written there.

God gi'-good-e'en.[2] I pray sir, can you read?

Ay, mine own fortune in my misery.[3]

Later that day, Lord Capulet gives his servant a list of people to invite to the masquerade.

Unfortunately, the servant can't read.[1] He heads off in search of someone who can.

Romeo and Benvolio, who are still discussing Romeo's broken heart, bump into the servant. He asks them for help.

Whither[4] should they come?

My master is the great rich Capulet, and if you be not of the house of Montagues, I pray come and crush a cup of wine.[5]

Compare her face with some that I shall show...

...And I will make thee think thy swan a crow.

Romeo reads the letter. He's impressed by the guest list – Rosaline is invited! He wonders who is throwing such a party.

The servant leaves. Benvolio tells Romeo to sneak into the feast, to see if his Rosaline matches up to other beauties attending.

One fairer than my love? The all-seeing sun ne'er[6] saw her match since first the world begun.

Nurse... Hear our counsel.[7]

Romeo doesn't believe there is anyone in the world prettier than Rosaline.

Meanwhile, in the Capulets' mansion, young Juliet talks to her mother, Lady Capulet, and her Nurse.[8]

1. can't read: in the 16th century only nobles and certain tradesmen were taught to read.
2. God gi'-good-e'en: God give you good evening. 3. Ay... misery: Romeo is making a grim joke about "reading," or realizing, the sadness in his own life. 4. Whither: to what place. 5. come... of wine: come for a drink.
6. ne'er: never. 7: counsel: discussion. 8. Nurse: the woman who helped bring Juliet up as a baby.

The three of them discuss Juliet's marriage to Paris. Lady Capulet asks the Nurse to persuade Juliet that Paris is a fine match.

The Nurse proudly says she knows exactly how old Juliet is – she isn't fourteen yet.

The Nurse hugs Juliet affectionately as she remembers breast-feeding her as a baby.[3]

Hearing enough, Lady Capulet impatiently asks the Nurse to be quiet and gets to the heart of the matter: Does Juliet want to marry?

Lady Capulet is determined to get an answer from Juliet. The marriage is important to the family because Paris is related to the Prince of Verona, but she also wants Juliet to be happy.

Juliet hardly knows her future husband, but she agrees to take a good look at Paris during the feast to see if she could grow to love him.

1. Thou knowest… age: You know she's a good age to marry.   2. Lammas-tide: August 1st, the harvest festival.
3. breast-feeding: it was once common for noble women to have servants, called wet nurses, to feed their babies.
4. How stands… married: How do you feel about getting married?
5. valiant: brave, noble.   6. He's a flower… flower: He's good-looking – very good-looking!

LOVE AT FIRST SIGHT

Evening comes and the Capulet masquerade begins.

> I am not for this ambling.[1]

> Nay, gentle Romeo, we must have you dance.

Outside in the street, an unhappy Romeo follows Benvolio and their friend Mercutio to Lord Capulet's house.

> Come, knock and enter; and no sooner in but every man betake him to his legs.[2]

> I'll be a candle-holder and look on; The game was ne'er so fair, and I am done.[3]

> Tut! Dun's the mouse,[4] the constable's own word![5]

They put on their masks, but Romeo isn't sure if he wants to go. Benvolio tries to encourage him to have some fun.

As they reach the Capulet mansion, Romeo offers to hold the torch and watch while the others enjoy themselves.

Mercutio warns the others to fade into the crowd – Montagues are not welcome here.

> I dreamt a dream tonight.

> And so did I.

> Well, what was yours?

> That dreamers often lie.

> Supper is done, and we shall come too late.

Romeo is worried – he had a dream that something bad will happen if they enter.

Mercutio laughs at Romeo, saying he shouldn't worry about dreams – they don't mean anything.

Worried that they will miss the party, Benvolio pushes the others through the door to the Capulet mansion.

---

1. ambling: dancing.   2. every man… legs: let's all get on the dance floor.   3. The game… done: I'm going to give up while the going is good.   4. Dun's the mouse: Mercutio is playing with Romeo's last word, "done." "Dun" means dark and brown, like a mouse, so he's comparing Romeo to a quiet mouse.   5. the constable's own word: a policeman always tells his men to be quiet when catching a criminal – don't get caught at the party!

They walk toward the busy banquet hall. Servants are running this way and that, shouting at each other.

As the three friends enter the Great Chamber, they see Lord Capulet welcoming his guests.

Capulet likes to see his guests dancing, but he feels too old to join in.

Meanwhile, Romeo sees Juliet from across the room, as she takes her mask off. He falls in love on the spot, without even knowing Juliet's name.

In a trance, Romeo has already forgotten his former love, Rosaline.

However, Tybalt, Lord Capulet's nephew, recognizes Romeo. Furious, he orders his servant to bring him his sword.

Lord Capulet wonders what is going on. Tybalt tells him he has seen Romeo, and is determined to start a fight.

Though Capulet holds him back, Tybalt swears to take revenge for their intrusion.

1. Great Chamber: main dining room. 2. she hangs… ear: she lights up the night like a sparkling jewel hanging next to black African skin. 3. Forswear it: Deny it. 4. rapier: a long, thin sword. 5. Wherefore storm you so?: Why are you so angry? 6. foe: enemy. 7. This intrusion… gall: Crashing the party may seem like fun now, but the Montagues will bitterly regret it.

THE LOVERS MEET

> My lips, two blushing pilgrims,[1] ready stand to smooth that rough touch with a tender kiss.

Unaware of the threat from Tybalt, Romeo boldly takes Juliet's hand and leads her to a quiet spot away from the other guests. He apologizes for his roughness.

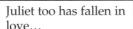

Juliet too has fallen in love…

> Good pilgrim, you do wrong your hand too much… palm to palm is holy palmer's[2] kiss.[3]

> Let lips do what hands do!

Lost in each other, the two young lovers kiss, then kiss again.

> You kiss by th' book.[4]

> Madam, your mother craves a word[5] with you.

Just then, the Nurse interrupts them with a message from Juliet's mother, Lady Capulet.

Reluctantly, Juliet tears herself away, leaving Romeo alone with the Nurse.

> What is her mother?

Romeo asks the Nurse who Juliet is. Her answer shocks him.

1. pilgrim: a visitor to a holy place – Romeo compares his lips to pilgrims as he worships Juliet's beauty. Romeo's name means "Pilgrim to Rome" in Italian.　2. palmer: pilgrims carried a palm leaf to show they had been to Jerusalem.　3. palm to… kiss: pilgrims touch hand to hand when they pray.　4. You kiss… book: You kiss like someone who has studied romantic novels – in other words, very well!　5. craves a word: wants to talk.

Her mother is the lady of the house.

Is she a Capulet? O dear account! My life is my foe's debt.[1]

Romeo is devastated. He realizes he's fallen head over heels in love with a Capulet, his family's bitter enemy.

Away, be gone, the sport is at the best.[2]

Ay, so I fear; the more is my unrest.[3]

Hearing the sound of footsteps, Romeo looks up. It's Benvolio. Now that Romeo knows who Juliet is, he's happy to leave the party.

I thank you, honest gentlemen. Good night.

Seeing them leave, Lord Capulet bids them good-bye.

Benvolio, Romeo, and Mercutio leave the Capulet mansion.

Come on, let's to bed.

Inside, Lord Capulet realizes how late it is and heads upstairs with Lady Capulet.

What's he that follows there, that would not dance?

His name is Romeo, and a Montague, the only son of your great enemy.

My only love, sprung from my only hate!

Too early seen unknown, and known too late.[4]

Juliet is keen to know who her handsome stranger is. Her Nurse tells her he is a Montague. Juliet realizes she has fallen for someone that she is supposed to hate.

1. Oh dear… debt: There's a terrible price to pay because I'm dependent on my enemy.
2. the sport… best: the best part of the party is over.
3. the more… unrest: if only you knew why I'm so worried.
4: Too early… late: I saw him too soon as a stranger, and I found out too late who he was.

THE BALCONY

Romeo has fallen in love again – but unlike Rosaline, Juliet loves him in return. Yet, what future can there be for the young lovers when their families are at war?

But Romeo can't get Juliet out of his head. He has to see her again… whatever the risk.

It's still dark when the three friends leave the feast. Romeo drops behind and leaps over the wall into the Capulet orchard.

Benvolio and Mercutio peer over the wall to see where Romeo has gone. Mercutio teases him, hoping Romeo will reveal his hiding place.

When Romeo doesn't appear, Benvolio persuades Mercutio to leave him alone. Mercutio agrees and they merrily head for home.

Romeo hears every word from inside the Capulet orchard. To him, Mercutio's mocking words show he has never been in love.

Creeping nearer the Capulet mansion, Romeo spies Juliet in a window above.

As he watches, Juliet comes out onto her balcony and speaks out loud,[7] not realizing that Romeo can hear from below.

---

1. conjure: to call up a spirit by saying magic words.   2. befits: suits.   3. 'Tis in… found: It's useless to seek someone who doesn't want to be found.   4. He jests… wound: He laughs because he has never felt the pain of being in love.
5. yonder window: that window (over there).   6. But soft… sun: Romeo imagines Juliet is the sun, rising in the east and spreading its soft light.   7. speaks out loud: in plays, a speech made when someone is alone is called a soliloquy.

O Romeo, Romeo, wherefore[1] art thou Romeo?

Deny thy father and refuse thy name.

What's in a name?

That which we call a rose by any other name would smell as sweet.[2]

Call me but love and I'll be new baptised;[3] henceforth[4] I never will be Romeo.

Juliet wishes Romeo could give up his family name. If he can't, she will happily change hers so they can be together.

Romeo calls out from the shadows.

Art thou not[5] Romeo, and a Montague?

If they do see thee, they will murder thee.

I have night's cloak to hide me from their eyes.

Dost thou[6] love me? I know thou wilt say "Ay" and I will take thy word.[7]

Juliet is suprised by the voice, but she guesses who it is in the dark.

Juliet warns Romeo about the danger, but Romeo is confident the darkness will keep him safe.

O wilt thou leave me so unsatisfied?

What satisfaction canst thou have tonight?

The exchange of thy love's faithful vow for mine.

I gave thee mine before thou didst request it![8]

Parting is such sweet sorrow[9] that I shall say goodnight 'til it be morrow.

Juliet must say good-bye, but Romeo climbs the balcony.

Romeo asks Juliet to marry him – she says yes! But for now Romeo must leave. They arrange to meet the next day.

It is almost dawn. Juliet can't bear to say good-bye – it feels like twenty years until tomorrow.

1. wherefore: why – why of all people is Romeo a Montague?   2. That which... sweet: A name means nothing – a rose still smells sweet whatever it is called – Romeo is still Romeo whatever his name is.   3. Call me... baptised: Say you love me and I will take a new name.   4. henceforth: from now on.   5. Art thou not: Aren't you.   6. Dost thou: do you.
7. thou wilt... word: you'll say yes and I'll believe you.   8. I gave... request it: I have already given you my love.
9. Parting is...sorrow: I'm sad to say good-bye but happy that it's you I'm talking to.

A VISIT TO THE FRIAR

Romeo hurries to see his friend Friar Laurence, an expert in making poisons and medicines from plants.

This being tasted, slays all senses with the heart.[1]

Good morrow, father.

Benedicite![2] Where hast thou been?

The Friar is surprised to see Romeo up so early and wonders what he has been up to. He suspects that Romeo must be worrying about something – or he'd still be in bed!

I have been feasting with mine enemy.

My heart's dear love is set on the fair daughter of rich Capulet.

This I pray, that thou consent[3] to marry us today.

Romeo tells the Friar all about meeting Juliet the night before. He begs the Friar to marry them right away!

Is Rosaline, that thou did love so dear, so soon forsaken?[4]

I pray thee chide[5] me not.

The Friar is shocked that Romeo has forgotten Rosaline so quickly.

I'll thy assistant be, for this alliance may so happy prove to turn your households' rancor to pure love.[6]

The Friar agrees to help, if only because he hopes their marriage will end the feud between the two families.

O let us hence![7]

Wisely and slow. They stumble that run fast.

Romeo is in a terrible rush, but the Friar warns him to take things slowly to avoid trouble.

---

1. This being… heart: When swallowed, this flower stops your heart – dead.
2. Benedicite: bless you! 3 consent: agree.   4. forsaken: forgotten, given up.   5: chide: scold, tell off.
6. this alliance… love: this marriage may be so fortunate that it will turn the hatred between the two families to love.
7. let us hence: let's get going.

Alas, poor Romeo, he is already dead.

Later that morning...

Mercutio and Benvolio wonder where Romeo is. Tybalt has challenged their friend to a duel.

Mercutio explains...

Why, what is Tybalt?

More than Prince of Cats,[1] I can tell you.

The very butcher of the silk button,[2] a duellist, a duellist!

What counterfeit[3] did I give you?

The slip, sir, the slip![4]

Not long after, Romeo turns up. Mercutio and Benvolio tease him for getting away from them the night before.

Farewell, ancient lady, farewell!

The three are still chatting when the Nurse arrives to meet Romeo, as planned. When Mercutio leaves with Benvolio, he makes fun of the Nurse.

I am so vexed[5] that every part about me quivers. Scurvy knave![6]

The Nurse is furious at Mercutio's bold remark. Romeo leads her to a quiet corner of the piazza to explain his plan.

Bid her devise some means to come to shrift[7] this afternoon.

And there she shall at Friar Laurence's cell be shrived[8] and married.

Romeo's servant will bring a rope ladder for the Nurse to smuggle into the Capulet mansion, so he can reach Juliet's room that night.

Commend[9] me to thy lady.

Ay, a thousand times.

The Nurse leaves to tell Juliet of the plan. Romeo calls after her.

1. Prince of Cats: Tybalt was the name of the cat in the medieval tale of Reynard the Fox.
2. butcher of the silk button: he slices through clothes like a butcher through meat!   3: counterfeit: fake, fraud.
4: The slip: a fake coin – Mercutio is playing with words when he says Romeo has given them the slip (run away from them).   5. vexed: angry.   6. Scurvy knave: Bold rascal.   7. Bid her...shrift: Tell her to find an excuse to make a confession (with the Friar).   8. shrived: forgiven for her sins.   9. Commend: Remember me kindly, recommend me.

THE MARRIAGE

Back in the Capulet mansion, Juliet waits for news of Romeo.

What haste! Do you not see that I am out of breath?

O honey nurse, what news? Hast thou[1] met with him?

When the Nurse enters, Juliet jumps up excitedly to talk to her.

What says he of our marriage?

Lord, how my head aches!

The Nurse teases Juliet by delaying her answer, but Juliet is impatient to know the plan.

Come, what says Romeo?

Have you got leave to go to shrift[2] today?

At last, the Nurse tells all.

I have.

Then hie[3] you hence[4] to Friar Laurence's cell: there stays a husband to make you a wife.

Hie to high fortune! Honest Nurse, farewell.

Juliet sets off for Friar Laurence's cell immediately.

Romeo waits for Juliet in Friar Laurence's cell…

So smile the heavens upon this holy act, that after-hours with sorrow chide us not![5]

Friar Laurence prays that their marriage won't bring trouble.

Love-devouring[6] death do what he dare — it is enough I may but call her mine.

Romeo answers that as long as he marries Juliet, he doesn't care what happens.

---

1. Hast thou: Have you.   2: shrift: confession (confessing your sins to a priest).   3. hie you: hurry.
4: hence: from here.   5. So smile... us not: God bless this marriage so that afterwards nothing goes wrong.
6: devouring: eating, consuming.

Here comes the lady. O, so light a foot will ne'er wear out the everlasting flint.[1]

Good even to my ghostly confessor.[2]

Just then, Juliet appears at the door.

Ah, Juliet, if the measure of thy joy be heaped like mine...

then sweeten with thy breath this neighbor air.[3]

Let rich music's tongue unfold the imagined happiness

that both receive in either by this dear encounter.[4]

My true love is grown to such excess I cannot sum up sum of half my wealth.[5]

Romeo steps forward, takes Juliet's hand lovingly, and looks deep into her eyes. Like Romeo, Juliet is overcome with emotion.

Come, come with me, and we will make short work.

The Friar knows time is of the essence, and promises to marry them as quickly as possible.

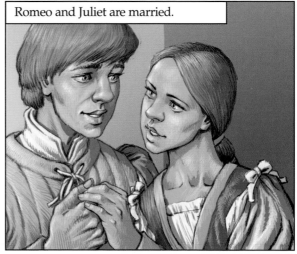

Romeo and Juliet are married.

1. so light… flint: Juliet walks so lightly she will never wear out the hard ground.   2: ghostly confessor: spiritual priest (who listens to confessions).   3. if the measure… air: if your joy is piled as high as mine, then sweeten the air with your words.
4. Let rich… encounter: Let your tongue speak words that talk of the happiness we both expect in getting married.
5. My true… wealth: My love for you has grown so great I can't add up half of how much I feel for you.

TROUBLE IN THE AIR

Later that day…

The day is hot, the Capulets abroad,[1] and, if we meet, we shall not 'scape a brawl.

Thou art as hot a Jack in thy mood as any in Italy.

Am I like such a fellow?

Mercutio and Benvolio are again in the piazza. It's a scorching hot day. Benvolio knows it's the sort of weather that brings trouble.

Mercutio laughs, saying Benvolio is as hot-tempered as anyone.

Benvolio steps back and gasps, pretending to be shocked by Mercutio's comments.

Thou wilt quarrel with a man that hath a hair more or a hair less in his beard than thou hast.

Mercutio continues…

By my head, here come the Capulets.

By my heel, I care not.

Benvolio spies a group of Capulets coming their way, led by Tybalt, Juliet's cousin.

Follow me close, for I will speak to them.

Tybalt is still furious that Romeo attended Capulet's feast and is looking to fight a duel with Romeo.

Mercutio, thou consortest with Romeo.[2]

Consort?[3] What, dost thou make us minstrels?[4] Here's my fiddlestick;[5] here's that shall make you dance.

Tybalt approaches Mercutio and Benvolio – he knows they are friends with Romeo.

Pointing to his sword, Mercutio makes fun of Tybalt – but there's a threat behind his teasing.

---

1. abroad: about. 2. consortest with: here it means "are friends with."
3. consort: here it means "a band of musicians." Mercutio deliberately misunderstands Tybalt to annoy him.
4. minstrels: hired musicians. 5. fiddlestick: here he means his sword.

24

Here all eyes gaze on us.

Well, peace be with you, sir. Here comes my man.

Romeo, the love I bear thee can afford no better reason than this:[1]

Thou art a villain.

Let them gaze. I will not budge for no man's pleasure, I.

Benvolio tries to stop the fight. Just then, Romeo arrives, so Tybalt leaves Mercutio alone.

Tybalt turns and challenges Romeo.

Villain am I none. Therefore farewell. I see thou knowest me not.

Boy, this shall not excuse the injuries that thou hast done me.

Good Capulet, which name I tender as dearly as mine own, be satisfied.

Therefore turn and draw.

Romeo turns and is ready to leave when Tybalt grabs his shoulder and spins him around.

Romeo wants to explain he has just married Juliet – but he can't. Now that he's related to Tybalt, he has no wish to fight him.

Tybalt, you ratcatcher, will you walk?[2]

What wouldst thou have with me?

They fight…

Good King of Cats, nothing but one of your nine lives.[3]

I am for you!

Tybalt is ready to leave Romeo alone when hot-headed Mercutio, disgusted that Romeo is not defending himelf, draws his sword and steps toward Tybalt, who rises to the bait.

1. The love I… than this: I can't say any better than this.   2. will you walk: do you refuse to fight?
3. nine lives: cats are often said to have "nine lives" because of their good survival skills.

THE DUEL

They cut and thrust…

"Hold,[1] Tybalt, Good Mercutio!"

Desperate to stop the fight, Romeo steps between the two men.

Seeing his opportunity, Tybalt thrusts under Romeo's arm.

"I am hurt. A plague on both your houses.[2]"

Tybalt stabs Mercutio, who staggers back, clutching at the wound in his chest.

"Ay, ay, a scratch, a scratch.[3]"

"What, are you hurt?"

As Romeo supports the wounded Mercutio in his arms, Benvolio runs over to help.

"A plague on both your houses!"

"Why the devil came you between us? I was hurt under your arm."

"I thought it for the best."

Mercutio blames Romeo for getting in the way.

"Help me into a house, Benvolio, or I shall faint… They have made worms' meat[4] of me."

Benvolio drags Mercutio to a nearby house where he can lie down until the doctor comes.

"My very[5] friend hath got this mortal hurt in my behalf.[6]"

Romeo blames himself for the fight and Mercutio's fatal wound.

1. Hold: Stop.   2. A plague… houses: A curse on both Montagues and Capulets.
3. a scratch: Mercutio is pretending it's not a bad wound.   4: worms' meat: a corpse.   5. very: true.
6. My friend… behalf: My friend has got this deadly injury because of me.

O Romeo, Romeo, brave Mercutio is dead!

Mercutio's soul is but a little way above our heads, staying for thine to keep him company.[1]

Either thou, or I, or both must go with him!

A minute later, Benvolio comes rushing out of the house, with grim news.

Romeo sees that Tybalt is still standing nearby. His blood boils. Drawing his sword, he attacks.

Romeo, away, be gone! The Prince will doom thee death[2] if thou art taken.

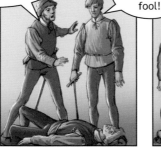

O, I am fortune's fool!

Benvolio, who began this bloody fray?[3]

Romeo runs Tybalt through with his sword and kills him.

Benvolio warns Romeo the Prince will execute him, so Romeo runs away.

Soon after, the Prince arrives, along with Lords Montague and Capulet and their wives.

Romeo, he cries aloud, "Hold, friends! Friends, part!" This is the truth, or let Benvolio die.

Romeo slew[4] Tybalt; Romeo must not live.

And for that offense immediately we do exile[5] him hence.

Benvolio explains that Romeo tried to stop the fighting, and only attacked Tybalt in revenge for Mercutio's death.

Lady Capulet says they can't trust Benvolio because he is related to Romeo. She wants bloody revenge.

The Prince, sad that his relative Mercutio has died, decides to banish Romeo from the city.

1. Mercutio... company: Mercutio's soul has not gone to heaven because he is waiting to see Tybalt killed in revenge.
2. doom thee death: condemn you to death.   3. fray: brawl.   4. slew: killed.   5. exile: banish.

BANISHED!

Come, loving, black-browed[1] night, give me my Romeo.

Why dost thou wring thy hands?

He's killed, he's dead.

If he be slain, say "Ay," if not, say "No."

O Tybalt, the best friend I had.

Meanwhile...

Juliet is in her room, alone. She can't wait for night – and her beloved Romeo – to arrive.

Hearing footsteps, Juliet jumps up in excitement – Romeo will soon be with her. But the Nurse brings terrible news...

Juliet is stunned – she thinks the Nurse is talking about Romeo.

Juliet is still confused.

Romeo that killed him, he is banished.

That villain cousin would have killed my husband.

Is Romeo slaughtered, and is Tybalt dead? My dearest cousin, and my dearer lord?[2]

O serpent heart, hid with a flowering face.[3]

At first Juliet blames Romeo, but then she realizes he may have had no choice.

I'll find Romeo to comfort you. He is hid at Laurence's cell.

"Romeo is banished": To speak that word is father, mother, Tybalt, Romeo, Juliet, all slain, all dead.

Give this ring to my true knight and bid him come to take his last farewell.

Juliet weeps as she realizes she may never see Romeo again – for her, a fate worse than death.

The Nurse hands Juliet the rope ladder and promises to fetch Romeo. In return, Juliet hands Nurse her ring as a token for Romeo.

1. black-browed: dark. 2. lord: husband. 3: serpent... face: Juliet is comparing Romeo to a snake, hiding in beautiful flowers – he has deceived her.

Father, what news?

Ha! Banishment! Be merciful, say "death."

This is dear mercy.[1]

I come from Lady Juliet. For Juliet's sake, rise and stand!

Hence from Verona thou art banished.

'Tis torture, not mercy.

Meanwhile, Romeo is hiding in Friar Laurence's cell.

When Romeo groans in despair, the Friar tries to comfort him.

They hear a knock. Terrified, Romeo hides himself. The Nurse enters and sees Romeo cowering.

Spak'st thou[2] of Juliet? How is it with her? Doth she not think me an old[3] murderer?

O, she says nothing, sir, but weeps and weeps.

In desperation, Romeo tries to stab himself with a knife, but the Nurse snatches the dagger away.

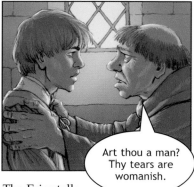

How well my comfort is revived by this![5]

The Friar explains…

Art thou a man? Thy tears are womanish.

The Friar tells Romeo to pull himself together – he has a plan!

The Friar will arrange for Romeo to go to Mantua[4] and then try to persuade the Prince to pardon him. Romeo can spend the night with Juliet, but must leave early to avoid capture. Romeo cheers up at the thought of seeing Juliet.

1. This is… mercy: Being banished is an act of mercy – you could have been executed.
2. Spak'st thou: Did you speak?   3. old: hardened.   4. Mantua: a neighboring town.
5. How well… this: This visit has really cheered me up.

A Sad Farewell

Unaware that Juliet has married Romeo, Lord Capulet is busy arranging Juliet's wedding with Paris. Meanwhile, Romeo has climbed up into Juliet's room to spend the night with her.

Morning breaks...

But time passes quickly, and soon Romeo must leave. He climbs out of Juliet's window.

Juliet goes back into her room, just as her mother enters. Afraid that she may never see Romeo again, she can't stop crying.

Lady Capulet thinks that Juliet's tears are for her slain cousin.

Lady Capulet promises revenge for Tybalt's death. Juliet has to pretend that she wants vengeance too.

30

1. A Thursday: On Thursday.   2. Yond: Yonder, over there.   3. Let me… wilt it: I don't mind being caught and executed if that's what you want.   4. The day is broke: It is daybreak.   5. Then, window… out: Then let the light in and let my beloved leave.   6. Evermore… death: Are you still crying over Tybalt's death?   7. behold: see.
8. I… dead: Juliet's words have a double meaning – she's also saying, "As long as Romeo lives, I can't get enough of him."

Marry, my child, early next Thursday morn.

I will not marry yet. And when I do, I swear, it shall be Romeo, whom you know I hate,[1] rather than Paris.

Hang thee, young baggage![2] Disobedient wretch!

I tell thee what — Get thee to church a Thursday or never after look me in the face.

Lady Capulet breaks the news that her father wants Juliet to marry Paris — in just three days. Juliet bluntly refuses, saying it is too soon after Tybalt's death.

When Lord Capulet hears Juliet's reply, he flies into a rage.

Lord Capulet disowns Juliet.

You are too hot.[4]

And you be mine I'll give you to my friend; and you be not[3] — hang! Beg! Starve! Die in the streets!

For by my soul I'll never acknowledge thee.

O Nurse, how can this be prevented? Hast thou not a word of joy?

After her parents leave, Juliet asks her Nurse for advice.

Romeo is banished. I think you are happy with this second match, for it excels your first.

Speakst thou from the heart?

And from my soul too.

O most wicked fiend! I'll to the Friar to know his remedy.[5] If all else fail, myself have power to die.

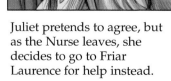

But instead of giving Juliet hope, the Nurse suggests she forget all about Romeo and marry Paris instead. Juliet is shocked.

Juliet pretends to agree, but as the Nurse leaves, she decides to go to Friar Laurence for help instead.

1. And when I do... hate: Juliet is making it sound like she'd rather marry anyone but Paris, when actually all she wants is Romeo.   2. baggage: immoral woman.   3. And you be mine... be not: If you're really my daughter, I'll give you to Paris, but if you're not...   4. hot: angry.   5. remedy: solution, plan.

FRIAR LAURENCE'S PLAN

On Thursday, sir? The time is very short.

Now, sir, her father counts it dangerous that she do give her sorrow too much sway,

and in his wisdom hastes our marriage.

Juliet hurries to see Friar Laurence, not knowing that Paris is visiting the Friar to arrange their marriage. But the Friar is trying to delay the ceremony, knowing full well he has already married Juliet to Romeo.

Paris explains that Juliet's father is keen to speed up the marriage because he is worried that Juliet is so upset at Tybalt's death.

I wish I knew not why it should be slowed.

Happily met, my lady and my wife!

The Friar tries to look pleased for Paris, but is secretly worried about what will happen when Capulet finds out about Juliet's marriage to Romeo.

At that moment, Juliet appears, looking flustered. Paris is delighted that she has turned up, thinking it a happy coincidence.

That may be, sir, when I may be a wife.

That "may be" must be, love, on Thursday next.

What must be, shall be.

Juliet, on Thursday I will rouse[1] ye.

Till then, adieu,[2] and keep this holy kiss.

Juliet wants to talk to the Friar about Romeo but can't say a thing with Paris there. Paris is eager to talk about the wedding, but Juliet is reluctant.

Finally, to get rid of Paris, Juliet pretends she has come to make her confession. Paris leaves so she can be alone with the Friar.

1. rouse: wake up.   2. adieu: farewell.

O, shut the door and when thou hast done so, come weep with me — past hope, past cure, past help!

If in thy wisdom thou canst not help... with this knife I'll help it presently.[1]

Hold, daughter, I do spy a kind of hope.

Once Paris has gone, Juliet bursts into tears.

Juliet is so upset that she threatens to kill herself with a dagger.

The Friar calms Juliet down and takes the knife from her.

Take thou this vial,[2] being then in bed, and this distilling liquor[3] drink thou off.

When the bridegroom in the morning comes to rouse thee from thy bed, there art thou dead.[4]

In the meantime, against shalt thou awake,[6] shall Romeo by my letters know our drift,[7] and hither shall he come.

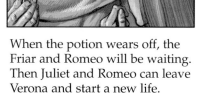

The Friar reveals his plan: the night before her wedding to Paris, she must swallow a potion that will make her look dead.

When Paris finds her everyone will think she's dead and she'll be buried in the family vault.[5]

When the potion wears off, the Friar and Romeo will be waiting. Then Juliet and Romeo can leave Verona and start a new life.

Give me, give me! O tell not me of fear!

I'll send a Friar with speed to Mantua, with my letters to thy lord.

Love, give me strength! Farewell, dear Father.[8]

Juliet takes the vial. The Friar warns her the potion is not for the fainthearted.

The Friar promises that he will send a messenger to Romeo so that he will know the plan.

Juliet thanks him and leaves, clutching the potion in her hand.

1. with this knife... presently: if you can't help me, I'll stab myself with this knife.   2. vial: bottle.
3. distilling liquor: drink that spreads through a body.   4. there art thou dead: you will seem dead.
5. vault: tomb.   6. against... awake: to be ready when you wake.   7. drift: plan.   8. Father: Catholic priest.

THE VIAL OF POTION

Juliet returns home. Falling to her knees, she pretends she is happy to marry Paris.

At this, Lord Capulet decides to move the wedding ahead one day. He tells the Nurse that Juliet is to be married the next day!

Later, as she gets ready for bed, Juliet asks the Nurse if she can be alone.

Juliet, still dressed, sits alone on her bed. Scared but determined, she takes out the vial of potion. She is terrified that it might kill her rather than just make her sleep deeply.

Juliet is worried she might wake up in the tomb alone, next to Tybalt's body. Despite this, she drinks the potion.

Downstairs, unaware of what is happening, Lord and Lady Capulet are busy preparing for the wedding feast.

1. Pardon… by you: Please forgive me, from now on I'll do as you say.
2. Make haste: Hurry up!

The next morning…

How sound is she asleep. I needs must wake her.

Alas! alas! Help! help! My lady's dead.

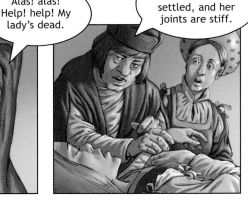

She's cold, her blood is settled, and her joints are stiff.

The potion does its work. Juliet is in a very deep sleep when the Nurse comes to wake her.

When the Nurse feels Juliet's stiff, cold body, she screams in horror.

Juliet's mother and father rush into her room. They're shocked by what they find – everyone thinks Juliet is dead.

Come, is the bride ready to go to church?

Ready to go,[1] but never to return.

My child is dead, and with my child my joys are buried.

Paris and the Friar enter the room. Paris looks on in horror as Lord and Lady Capulet weep over Juliet's body.

Playing his part, the Friar gently persuades Capulet to place Juliet's body in the family vault. So far the plan is working well.

Meanwhile, in Mantua...

How now, Balthasar. How fares my Juliet?

Her body sleeps in Capel's[2] monument.

Is it e'en so?[3] Then I defy you, stars.[4] Hast thou no letters to me from the Friar?

No, my good lord.

No matter. Get thee gone and hire those horses.

But tragedy strikes! The Friar's messenger never reaches Romeo, as a plague prevents him from entering Mantua. Romeo knows nothing of the Friar's plan! He hears from his servant Balthasar only that Juliet is dead. Romeo can't believe his ears.

Romeo makes plans to return to Verona. He will visit Juliet in the tomb that night.

1. Ready to... return: Ready to be buried.   2. Capel: the Capulet family.
3. Is it e'en so?: Can this really be true?   4. stars: fate, destiny.

THE TOMB

Well, Juliet, I will lie with thee tonight.

After Balthasar leaves...

Romeo breaks down and weeps for Juliet. He decides to kill himself rather than live without her.

Romeo visits an apothecary[1] to buy some poison.

Hold, there is forty ducats.[2] Let me have a dram[3] of poison.

My poverty, but not my will[4] consents.

I pay thy poverty and not thy will.

Come, cordial[5] and not poison, go with me to Juliet's grave.

Unhappy fortune! Friar John, go hence.

Get me an iron crow[6] and bring it straight unto my cell.

The Apothecary knows the law forbids him from selling poison, but he is poor and cannot resist Romeo's gold.

Poison in hand, Romeo heads to see Juliet, even though he has been banished from Verona.

Meanwhile, Friar Laurence hears that Romeo never received his message. He realizes he must free Juliet from the tomb.

Whistle then to me, as signal that thou hearest something approach.

What cursed foot wanders this way tonight?

That night...

Paris visits the tomb where Juliet's body lies. He tells his servant to warn him if anyone else enters the churchyard.

As Paris lays flowers on Juliet's tomb, he hears his page whistling: someone is coming!

It is Romeo, walking toward the tomb with a torch and a crowbar. He has ordered his servant Balthasar to leave him alone.

---

1. apothecary: someone who sells drugs or medicines.   2. ducats: gold coins.   3. dram: small amount.
4. will: conscience, sense of right and wrong.   5. cordial: medicine – it will relieve Romeo's pain.
6. crow: crowbar, a hooked iron bar used to force open doors.

Condemned villain, I do apprehend thee.[1]

Obey, and go with me, for thou must die.

Good gentle youth, tempt not a desperate man.[2]

Have at thee,[3] boy!

As Romeo forces open the tomb door with his crowbar, Paris steps forward. When he recognizes Romeo, he is furious.

Romeo tries to persuade Paris to leave him alone. But Paris refuses, so Romeo draws his sword and they fight.

If thou be merciful, open the tomb, lay me with Juliet.

Oh my love, my wife.

Death, that hath sucked the honey of thy breath, hath no power yet upon thy beauty.[4] Thou art not conquered.

As Paris lies dying, he has one final request.

Romeo carries Paris's body into the tomb and lays it down. In the flickering torchlight, he sees Juliet's body lying nearby. He gazes at her face one last time.

Beauty's ensign yet is crimson in thy lips and in thy cheeks,

and death's pale flag is not advanced there.[5]

Here's to my love! O true apothecary!

Thy drugs are quick. Thus, with a kiss, I die.

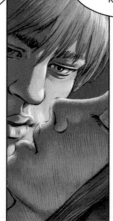

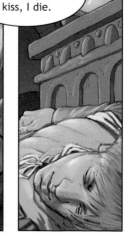

Though Romeo is surprised by Juliet's red cheeks and lips, he does not realize she is still alive.

1. Condemned… thee: You criminal, I arrest you.   2. tempt… man: don't push me as I'm desperate.
3. Have at thee: Take that!   4. Death… beauty: Death has taken your breath away, but not your beauty.
5. Beauty… there: Your lips and cheeks are still rosy – you haven't turned pale in death.

ALL ARE PUNISHED

Arriving at the tomb, the Friar meets Balthasar and hears that Romeo has gotten there first.

He notices a pool of blood from a fight. Dashing inside, he finds Romeo's pale body and Paris' bloody corpse.

Just then, Juliet awakes. The effects of the potion have worn off. Not seeing Romeo's dead body, she asks the Friar what has happened.

Hearing the Prince's men outside, the Friar tries to lead Juliet out of the tomb, but she refuses.

While the Friar makes his escape, Juliet sees the vial of poison in Romeo's hand.

Deciding to join Romeo in death, Juliet kisses his lips, hoping some of the poison will rub off.

The Prince's men are just outside, so Juliet decides to act quickly. Seizing Romeo's dagger, she plunges it into her chest and dies. Just then, the soldiers enter the tomb.

1. churl: a person with bad manners.
2. Drunk all…after?: You drank all the poison and left none to help me follow you?
3. This is…sheath: When I plunge this dagger into me, my body will become its sheath (covering).

"Hold him in safety until the Prince comes hither."

"Sovereign,[1] here lies the County Paris slain; and Romeo dead; and Juliet."

By now it is dawn.

"O heavens! O wife, look how our daughter bleeds!"

Two guards bring in the Friar and Balthasar, having captured them in the graveyard.

When the Prince arrives, along with Lord and Lady Capulet, the soldiers explain what has happened.

Lady Capulet screams and runs to hold Juliet, while Lord Capulet looks on in horror.

"My wife is dead tonight! Grief of my son's exile hath stopped her breath."

"Romeo, there dead, was husband to that Juliet; I married them."

"This letter he early bid me give his father."

Lord Montague enters, bringing news that his wife collapsed and died when she heard Romeo was banished.

The Friar explains all: Romeo and Juliet's secret marriage, the potion, and why Romeo killed himself when the letter did not reach him.

Balthasar tells how Paris and Romeo came to fight. He hands the Prince a letter Romeo wrote to his father.

"Capulet, Montague, see what a scourge is laid upon your hate.[2] All are punished."

"For never was a story of more woe than this of Juliet and her Romeo."

"As rich shall Romeo by his lady lie — poor sacrifices of our enmity.[3]"

After reading the letter, the Prince shames Lords Capulet and Montague for the tragedy they have brought upon themselves.

Montague and Capulet agree to end their family feud and erect a statue of the two lovers as a memorial.

The End

1. Sovereign: Ruler, lord.
2. see what... hate: see what a tragedy your hatred has brought.
3. poor sacrifices... enmity: our hatred cost their lives.

WILLIAM SHAKESPEARE (1564–1616)

William Shakespeare was born in Stratford-upon-Avon, Warwickshire, England, in 1564, possibly on April 23, which is St. George's Day – the feast-day of England's patron saint. His father was a respected businessman who became mayor of Stratford, though it seems he never learned to write. We know nothing of William's childhood and education, except that he did not go to university. He probably learned Latin at the King's New School in Stratford. In 1582 he married Anne Hathaway. He was only 18; she was 26, and pregnant. Their daughter Susanna was born six months later, and in 1585 they had twins, Hamnet and Judith. Anne and the children seem to have stayed in Stratford all their lives, even while William was living in London.

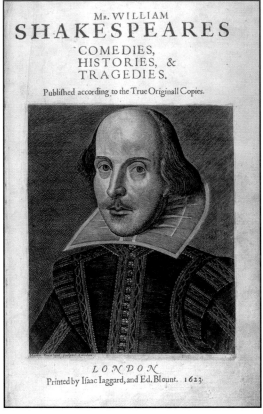

Portrait of Shakespeare by Martin Droeshout, on the title page of the First Folio edition of Shakespeare's plays (London, 1623).

LONDON AND THE THEATER

Shakespeare was acting and writing plays in London by about 1590. We do not know how he made his living before that, or how he got started as a playwright. London in the 1590s was an exciting place for anyone interested in the stage. Theaters – or "playhouses" – were not allowed in the City of London itself; they were built on the north side of London, outside the city walls, and in Southwark, on the south bank of the Thames. Many playwrights were active in London at this time. Christopher Marlowe wrote several blockbuster tragedies before being killed in a brawl at the age of 29. Other well-known writers included Thomas Dekker, Thomas Kyd, John Webster, Thomas Middleton, and the partnership of Francis Beaumont and John Fletcher. In the 1600s, Ben Jonson wrote a series of clever and witty comedies; Shakespeare acted in some of them.

Writing plays was not an especially well-paid job – the author's fee might be less than the value of an actor's costume. But Shakespeare was a keen businessman. In 1594 he became a shareholder in a new acting company, the Lord Chamberlain's Men. This meant that he invested money in the company, and in return he was paid a share of the profits made by the company.

Up to then, Shakespeare had worked in two theaters just outside the city walls in northeast London. Sometime after 1596, he moved south across the River Thames where he became manager of two theaters, the Rose and the Swan. With the money he made, he bought land in Stratford for his family, and a magnificent house – New Place. He also became a shareholder in the new Globe Theater, which opened in 1599.

A BIG SUCCESS

Shakespeare's name first appeared on his printed plays in 1598. That year, Francis Meres praised him as a playwright. This and other comments about his plays show that Shakespeare was highly regarded as a writer in his own time. In 1603 Queen Elizabeth I died and James VI of Scotland became James I of England. James really liked the theater, and he changed the name of the Lord Chamberlain's Men to the King's Men – Shakespeare and the other actors were now part of the royal household. The company was very successful and in 1608 it bought the Blackfriars Theatre, an indoor venue, to play to wealthier audiences. Shakespeare's plays were also performed at the royal court and in noble homes.

A cutaway view of the Globe Theater in Southwark, London, where many of Shakespeare's plays were first performed.
A copy of the Globe was completed in 1997, close to the original site, and Shakespeare's plays (among others) are regularly performed there.

After 1603, however, Shakespeare acted less and less, playing small roles such as the Ghost in *Hamlet*. In 1607, now 43 years old, he may have become ill due to exhaustion, and after this he wrote few plays. Around 1610 he seems to have retired from the theater and spent most of his time in Stratford. He died there on St. George's Day, 1616.

SHAKESPEARE'S WORKS

Shakespeare wrote about 39 plays (experts disagree about the exact number), four long poems, and 154 sonnets (short poems of 14 lines). Only about half his plays were published in his lifetime, but in 1623 two of his friends from the King's Men published a deluxe edition of 36 plays. This very valuable book is known today as the First Folio.

In the 400 years since he lived, Shakespeare has come to be regarded as the greatest playwright in the English language – perhaps in any language.

ROMEO AND JULIET

In perhaps his most famous play, *Romeo and Juliet*, Shakespeare created one of the greatest yet most tragic love stories ever told. Even people who have never read or seen the play know the names of the young lovers. Many of the play's lines are well known and newspaper headlines still use the word "Romeo" today to describe a male lover. The play was first published in 1597, but it was written down from memory by three of the actors who had performed the play. A much more accurate version was published two years later in 1599. These two versions were both printed as quartos, flimsy books that were made up of sheets of paper folded twice to make four leaves. Neither version was supervised by Shakespeare himself, so they don't always agree, and later versions create even more uncertainty – so modern editions of the play often differ from one another.

A BORROWED TALE

Like many other playwrights of the time, Shakespeare rarely invented the storylines for his plays, but borrowed them from earlier works. The tale of Romeo and Juliet was first written down by the Italian Masuccio Salernitano in 1476. Over the next hundred years, it was rewritten by several French and Italian authors.

In England the story of the two doomed lovers was well known thanks to a poem published in 1562 by Arthur Brooke, *The Tragicall Historye of Romeus and Juliet*.

This was the main source for Shakespeare's play, along with another version of the tale written by William Painter in 1567, *The goodly Historye of the true and constant love between Rhomeo and Julietta*. So even without Shakespeare's prologue (introduction), many of the audience would already know how the story would end – the thrill came from seeing how the plot unfolded. Shakespeare, however, made some big changes to Brooke's version which added to the drama. For example, Brooke's story stretches over nine months, but in Shakespeare's tale everything happens in just a few days: Romeo and Juliet fall in love instantly and almost right away things start to go horribly wrong, forcing them to take increasingly desperate action. Shakespeare also made characters such as Mercutio, the Nurse, and Tybalt much more important, adding to the drama and intrigue of the play.

PERFORMING THE PLAY

Though records are not entirely clear, the play was perhaps performed for the first time in 1595 at James Burbage's Theater, just outside the City of London. It was the first ever purpose-built playhouse. The Theater had an open stage and could hold about 3,000 people, with seating split over three levels and a cheaper standing area in the center for poorer audience members. It had several doors at the back of the stage, allowing the actors to make quick exits and appearances.

Shakespeare made his Juliet very young – just 13 years old – as it was common for young teenage girls to marry at the time the play is set (the Renaissance – see page 44). The part would have been played by a boy of the same age, since women were forbidden at that time from acting. Romeo may have been played by one of the young apprentices; the leader of the company, Richard Burbage, usually played the lead role in Shakespeare's plays, but he was 28 and would have appeared too old. Shakespeare may well have gone to rehearsals to give directions to the actors, working with a musician and a dancing instructor for the ball scenes and with Burbage in the fight scenes.

Tudor audiences loved violent plays and were fascinated by swordplay. Demonstrations of fencing were often seen on the stage alongside plays, so it's likely that many of the actors in *Romeo and Juliet* were also expert swordsmen. In 1598, Ben Jonson (a good friend of Shakespeare's) was arrested for duelling with and killing fellow actor Gabriel Spencer. Jonson got off with manslaughter rather than murder, and was punished by being branded with a "T" on his left thumb. But in 1613 King James I changed the law, so that anyone caught duelling could be punished by death – like the Prince's threat to execute any Montague or Capulet who "disturb our streets again."

WHAT THE CRITICS SAID

In 1662, writer Samuel Pepys saw the first production of the play since the restoration of Charles II to the throne after the English Civil War. He thought it was "the play of itself the worst that I ever heard in my life, and the worst acted I ever saw!"

In 1672, poet John Dryden was more kind, praising the play and in particular the character Mercutio: "Shakespear showed the best of his skill in his Mercutio, and he said himself, that he was forc'd to kill him in the third Act, to prevent being kill'd by him."

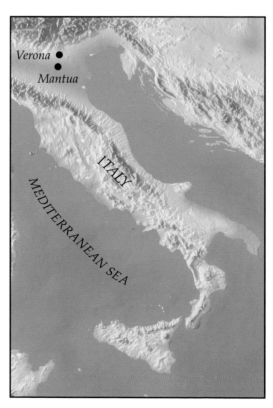

A modern-day map of Italy showing Verona and Mantua (called Mantova in Italian).

HISTORICAL BACKGROUND

It's not clear when *Romeo and Juliet* is meant to be set, but it seems to be some time during the Renaissance, a period that began in the 14th century and lasted until the early 17th century. The word "renaissance" means "rebirth" and refers to the European revival of the ideas of ancient Greece and Rome.

The English Renaissance reached its peak during the reign of Queen Elizabeth I (1558–1603). Adventurers such as Walter Raleigh and Francis Drake crossed the great oceans, and thinkers and scientists such as Francis Bacon and William Gilbert explored new ideas. After the defeat of the Spanish Armada in 1588, England's national pride grew. People's clothes, manners, and language all became more colorful, and all of this is reflected in Shakespeare's plays.

VIOLENT TIMES

During the Renaissance there were many changes in European society and politics. Italy was not a unified country but a group of city-states, each controlled by one or more powerful families. For example, the city of Florence was run by the Medici family, just as Shakespeare's Verona was ruled by Prince Escalus.

In the 14th century, Verona was a thriving trade city, but violence could flare up at any time. As in many other Italian city-states, a fierce rivalry existed in Verona between supporters of the Roman Catholic Pope and supporters of the Emperor. Fights could break out over petty differences in clothing or eating habits.

FAMILY FEUDS

Tudor England was also a violent place. During Shakespeare's time there was a well-known feud between the Danvers and Long families of England, which began when Charles and Henry Danvers killed their neighbor Henry Long. Some people have suggested that this rivalry might have been yet another source of inspiration for Shakespeare as he was writing *Romeo and Juliet*.

THE PLAGUE

Further tension was created by the constant threat of plague. From 1347 to 1349 the Black Plague wiped out a third of Europe's population, and in overcrowded cities like Verona plagues could spread rapidly. In *Romeo and Juliet*, Shakespeare acknowledges this threat when Friar Laurence's messenger is unable to reach Romeo due to the threat of a plague in Mantua.

BAD LUCK

Romeo and Juliet revolves around ideas of destiny, fate, and luck. During the Renaissance, many people believed that their lives were in the hands of God and Fate. In the 6th century AD, the Roman philosopher Boethius had tried to explain why tragedy happens in *The Consolation of Philosophy*. He proposed that people can't control their fate and that good or bad luck occurs at random. This is just what happens to Romeo and Juliet – forces beyond their control decide their unfortunate destiny.

Important Events
In England and Europe in Shakespeare's time

1475
Italian Masuccio Salernitano writes the original story of Romeo and Juliet.

1562
English poet Arthur Brooke publishes a poem called *The Tragicall Historye of Romeus and Juliet*, Shakespeare's main source for *Romeo and Juliet*.

1564
William Shakespeare is born in Stratford-upon-Avon, Warwickshire. Elizabeth I has been Queen of England since 1558.

1567
William Painter writes *The goodly Historye of the true and constant love between Rhomeo and Julietta*, another source for Shakespeare's version.

1576
First theater in England – "The Theatre" – built in London by the Earl of Leicester after fears that strolling actors might spread the plague.

1577
Francis Drake sets out to sail around the world on the *Golden Hind* (returns 1580). Alliance between England and Netherlands.

1582
Outbreak of plague in London. Shakespeare marries Anne Hathaway.

1583
Shakespeare's daughter Susanna born.

1584
Conspiracy against Elizabeth I involving Mary Queen of Scots.

1585
Shakespeare's children Hamnet and Judith (twins) born.

1587
Mary, Queen of Scots, convicted of plotting against Elizabeth I, is executed. Drake destroys Spanish ships in Cádiz harbor and claims to have "singed the king of Spain's beard."

1588
Spanish Armada of Philip II is defeated by the English fleet under Lord Howard of Effingham, Sir Francis Drake, and Sir John Hawkins.

1592
Earliest known reference to Shakespeare as a playwright. During this year a plague in London closes the theaters.

1594
Shakespeare is now a leader of the theater company, the Lord Chamberlain's Men.

1595
Shakespeare writes *Romeo and Juliet*. Probably the date of the play's first performance. By now, 15,000 people a week attend plays in London.

1597
Shakespeare buys and restores New Place in Stratford.

1598
Shakespeare's name first appears on the title pages of his printed plays.

1599
The Globe Theater opens in Southwark.

1603
Elizabeth I dies, aged 69. James VI of Scotland becomes James I of England. The Lord Chamberlain's Men become the King's Men.

1604
England and Spain make peace.

1605
The Gunpowder Plot, a Catholic conspiracy to assassinate James I and his Parliament, is foiled on November 5.

1608
The King's Men acquire Blackfriars Theater for performances during winter.

1610
Shakespeare retires from working in the theater.

1613
The Globe Theater burns down during a performance of Shakespeare's play *All Is True* (later called *Henry VIII*). It is quickly rebuilt.

1616
William Shakespeare dies in Stratford on April 23, at the age of 52. In the same year, English doctor William Harvey is first to describe the way blood flows through the body.

The first performance of *Romeo and Juliet* was not part of a long run, as is sometimes the case with new plays today, but was slotted into a program with other already popular works. However, even in Shakespeare's lifetime it became a big hit, and over the centuries it has remained one of Shakespeare's most performed plays.

In 1750, during the *"Romeo and Juliet war,"* rival productions ran at the Drury Lane and Covent Garden theaters in London. In 1845, Charlotte Cushman played Romeo (alongside her sister, who played Juliet) so well that Queen Victoria wrote, "No one would ever have imagined [Charlotte] was a woman." One of the most famous stagings of the last 100 years (in 1935) starred John Gielgud and Laurence Olivier as Romeo and Mercutio (they swapped roles after six weeks!) with Peggy Ashcroft as Juliet.

Sisters Charlotte and Susan Cushman playing Romeo and Juliet, 1845.

ON THE SILVER SCREEN

In all, some 300 versions of Shakespeare's plays have been filmed, and *Romeo and Juliet* is perhaps the most-screened play of all time. The first two versions were silent films, one (now lost) produced by French director Georges Méliès in 1902 for Thomas Edison, while an American version made in 1908 was filmed in Central Park in New York City.

In 1929, the first talking version was filmed as part of the Hollywood Revue, when John Gilbert and Norma Shearer acted out the famous balcony scene. The first major film version of the play was directed by George Cukor in 1932.

At huge expense, a replica of an Italian Renaissance city was built in a Hollywood studio, but the film was not a success. Audiences felt its stars, 34-year-old Norma Shearer (Juliet) and 42-year-old Leslie Howard (Romeo), were too old to play the teenage lovers.

In 1954 Italian director Renato Castellani won the Grand Prix at the Venice Film Festival for his version of *Romeo and Juliet*, which was filmed on location in a hilltop town in northern Italy. This paved the way for Franco Zeffirelli's 1968 version, which – though it cut more than half the original text – was full of color and energy and became a box office success. Zeffirelli used two teenage actors, Leonard Whiting and Olivia Hussey, to play the leads. Australian director Baz Luhrmann also cast teenagers in his 1996 movie *Romeo & Juliet*, starring Leonardo DiCaprio and Claire Danes.

Aimed at a younger audience, Luhrmann's film moves the setting from Renaissance Italy to Verona Beach, California in 2020. His Montagues and Capulets are warring business empires whose gang members fight with guns rather than swords.

OTHER VERSIONS

Romeo and Juliet has also been adapted many times for TV and film. In the 1961 musical, *West Side Story*, set in New York, the Montagues are the Jets, a gang of white youths, while the Capulets are the Sharks, a Puerto Rican gang.

In 2006, Disney borrowed the storyline in the first *High School Musical*, whose two young lovers are from rival high school groups.

The play has also been turned into poems, dramas, operas, orchestral and choral music, and ballets, as well as serving as the inspiration for many famous painters. In 1830 Italian composer Vincenzo Bellini wrote a famous opera based on *Romeo and Juliet* entitled *The Capulets and the Montagues*. In 1839 French composer Hector Berlioz wrote the dramatic *Romeo and Juliet* symphony. The best-known ballet *Romeo and Juliet* is by Russian composer Sergei Prokofiev, written in 1936.

OTHER PLAYS BY SHAKESPEARE

Note: We do not know the exact dates of most of Shakespeare's plays, or even the exact order in which they were written. The dates shown here are only approximate.

1590: *Henry VI, Part I*
1591: *Henry VI, Part II*
      Henry VI, Part III
1593: *Richard III*
1594: *Edward III**
      Titus Andronicus
      The Comedy of Errors
      The Taming of the Shrew
      The Two Gentlemen of Verona
1595: *Love's Labour's Lost*
      Richard II
      Romeo and Juliet
1596: *King John*
      A Midsummer Night's Dream
1597: *The Merchant of Venice*
      The Merry Wives of Windsor
      Henry IV, Part I
1598: *Henry IV, Part II*
1599: *Much Ado About Nothing*
      As You Like It
      Julius Caesar
      Henry V
      Hamlet

1602: *Twelfth Night*
1603: *All's Well That Ends Well*
1604: *Othello*
      Measure for Measure
1605: *King Lear*
1606: *Macbeth*
1608: *Pericles*
      Coriolanus
      Timon of Athens
      Troilus and Cressida
      Antony and Cleopatra
1610: *Cymbeline*
1611: *The Winter's Tale*
      The Tempest
1613: *Henry VIII***
1614: *The Two Noble Kinsmen***

Shakespeare probably wrote two other plays, *Love's Labour's Won* and *Cardenio*, which have not survived.

*May not be by Shakespeare
** By Shakespeare and John Fletcher

47

INDEX

A
adaptations 47

B
Burbage, Richard 43

E
Elizabeth I 41, 44, 45

F
films 46–47
First Folio 41

G
Globe Theater 41, 45

H
Hathaway, Anne 40, 45

I
Italy 43, 44, 46

J
James I 41, 43, 45
Jonson, Ben 40, 43
Juliet 42, 43, 44, 46

K
King's Men 41, 45

L
London 40, 41, 42, 45,
  46
Lord Chamberlain's
  Men 40, 41, 45

M
Marlowe, Christopher
  40
Mercutio 42, 43, 46
musicals 47

P
plague 44, 45
playwrights 40, 42

R
Renaissance 44
Roman Catholic
  Church 44
Romeo 42, 43, 44, 46

S
Spanish Armada 44, 45
Stratford-upon-Avon
  40, 41, 45

T
Theater, The 42, 45
theaters 40, 41, 42, 45,
  46

V
Verona 43, 44

W
works by Shakespeare
  41, 47

IF YOU LIKED THIS BOOK, YOU MIGHT ALSO WANT TO TRY THESE TITLES IN THE
BARRON'S *GRAPHIC CLASSICS* SERIES:

<table>
<tr><td>*Adventures of Huckleberry Finn*</td><td>*Macbeth*</td></tr>
<tr><td>*Dr. Jekyll and Mr. Hyde*</td><td>*The Man in the Iron Mask*</td></tr>
<tr><td>*Dracula*</td><td>*Moby Dick*</td></tr>
<tr><td>*Frankenstein*</td><td>*The Odyssey*</td></tr>
<tr><td>*Gulliver's Travels*</td><td>*Oliver Twist*</td></tr>
<tr><td>*Hamlet*</td><td>*A Tale of Two Cities*</td></tr>
<tr><td>*The Hunchback of Notre Dame*</td><td>*The Three Musketeers*</td></tr>
<tr><td>*Jane Eyre*</td><td>*Treasure Island*</td></tr>
<tr><td>*Journey to the Center of the Earth*</td><td>*20,000 Leagues Under the Sea*</td></tr>
<tr><td>*Julius Caesar*</td><td>*Wuthering Heights*</td></tr>
<tr><td>*Kidnapped*</td><td></td></tr>
</table>